The Lion's Share

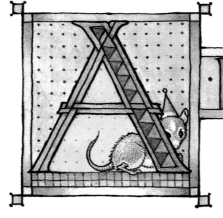 **LONG · TIME · AGO**

Leo Golden Mane ruled an empire of cats. The emperor couldn't read or write, not even his own name, but he didn't care. When he roared, everyone jumped.

Leo Golden Mane had a fancy palace, a beautiful wife, trunks full of gold, and only one worry. Rumor had it that another ruler, King Otto of the North, lived in a palace whose walls were lined with some unnamed treasure. "What could Otto of the North possibly have that I don't?" Leo Golden Mane fumed.

In time, a prince was born to the royal couple. Tiny wings sprouted from Prince Leo II's back. His nanny spotted them and told the empress, who told her husband. Leo Golden Mane narrowed his eyes for a minute and then he bellowed, "It's a blessing! Our son will go far!"

Then there was much rejoicing. Cats from all over the empire brought gifts to the newborn prince. The cougar gave him a ruby rose whose petals would never fade, and the Siamese gave a gleaming silver rattle.

Prince Leo II was raised with every luxury, but no storybooks and not one flying lesson, since birds wouldn't dare come to the palace. Even so, as Leo grew, so did his wings, and it felt good to stretch and flap them. One day, while gazing out an open window, he lifted his wings, caught a swift-moving breeze, and was gone.

He soon understood that there was more to flying than simply having wings.

"I wish I knew how to turn around," he thought . . .

"Or at least how to land." Leo struggled over land and sea, growing more and more lost and tired. Finally, he flew into a dense forest and—boom!—he crashed into a tree. Leo fell to the ground. A bear and an owl, returning home from a day of ice fishing, found him.

"What's a lion doing here?" exclaimed the bear. "How strange—I don't think they usually have wings."

"They don't," said the owl.

"I can't say that the lions have been friends to us," remarked the bear. "Quite the opposite. One thing's for certain, though, this little fellow needs our help."

So they bundled Leo into their sleigh and took him home with them.

"Where am I?" asked Leo.

"You are safe in my home. This is Owl, and I am King Otto of the North."

"Really?" said Leo. He was surprised at such a ramshackle place, but didn't want to hurt the bear's feelings. "My father is Leo Golden Mane, Emperor of the Cats. I'm Prince Leo II." He stared at the objects shelved from floor to ceiling. "What are those things?"

The bear smiled. "Those are my books. I'll read you a story from one of them later. But first things first. Let's get you patched up and fed."

Leo ate a big bowl of soup, while the bear and the owl bandaged his wing. Then he snuggled into bed.

Owl flew to the highest shelf and brought down a book for Otto. The bear opened it and began reading, "Once upon a time . . ." Leo listened and gazed at the pictures. When the story was finished, he reached out and turned the pages.

"Can I have another one?" he asked. Otto kept reading, story after story.

At last, Leo fell asleep.

When Leo woke up, the first words out of his mouth were "Please read me another story."

"Let me get you something to eat, and then, while you are resting, we'll teach you to read for yourself," said the bear.

Leo was a quick learner, but a slow healer. Friends stopped in to meet him, and they brought him treats and cheered him on as he got stronger. By the time he was out of bed, he could read almost any book on the shelves.

"I am so proud of you, Leo," said Otto.

"Now it's time to find out what those wings are for!" said Owl.

Leo learned to take off, soar, turn, brake, and land.

Now that spring had come, Leo flew every day and his wings grew very strong.

One afternoon, he landed on a high cliff and sat, watching the sea. That night Leo dreamed of his home. When he woke up, he said, "I think it's time to go back. My parents must be worried."

"Yes, Leo," Otto replied sadly. "It's time. Here's your favorite storybook to remember us by, and a map to get you home. Fly safely, little friend."

"And don't forget to brake with your feet," added Owl.

Leo hugged them both and started flying south. When he reached home, the lights were dim in the palace. The emperor and empress were still mourning their lost son.

Leo soared through the first window he could find.

"I'm home!" he shouted.

Leo Golden Mane started to scold Leo, but then he hugged him close. "Oh, Leo," he said. "We thought you were gone forever. Who has kept you safe all this time? How can I reward them?"

"King Otto of the North took care of me. And his friend . . ."

Before Leo could finish, Owl flew in and landed in their midst. "Great flying, Leo—I couldn't keep up with you," she panted. "This fell from your book." She handed Leo a letter. "It's important."

While the cats wondered at the book and peered at the letter, Prince Leo gave Owl some food and water. He told the others, "This brave owl helped save my life. Please make sure she is safe with us."

Then, since Leo was the only one in all the land who could read, he opened the letter and began:

Dear Leo,

A book is a treasure for sharing, so please read this one to your friends at home.

Remember that books are friends, too. They will help you rule with wisdom and true courage when that day comes.

You are always welcome here in the North, and we hope that one day we can visit your kingdom, too. Our families have always been enemies, but now that I know you, I see that it makes no sense at all. I hope you agree. We miss you.

King Otto of the North

Leo did as Otto said. He read the storybook to all
his friends.

And so it was that Leo Golden Mane and King Otto
of the North became friends, and Prince Leo would
one day rule a land filled with new treasures—books.

With thanks to the talented models Jack, Ozzie, Sherman, Tommy, and Zici, and their human friends Lisa Feingold and Sue Wall

Key to the Endpapers

A Androcles and the Lion

B Baba Yaga

C The Cook and the Mouse

D Dick Whittington and His Cat

E Eros and Psyche

F The Frog Princess

G The Genie and the Fisherman

H Hanukkah

I Icarus

J Jack Frost

K King Grisly-Beard

L Little Red Ridinghood

M The Magic Brocade

N Narcissus

O The Old Dame and Her Hen

P The People Who Could Fly

Q Queen Esther

R Rumpelstiltskin

S Sinbad the Sailor

T The Giant Turnip

U Urashima

V The Valiant Chatti-maker

W Wee Wee Mannie

X Xmas

Y The Young Head of the Family

Z Zeus